This book was made especially for:

❧ August ❧

Dear August,

You are *everything* to me! From your smile to your laugh to your giggles and toes, I simply can't imagine life without you. Here's a story to help you understand just how precious you are— and what Everything really means.

Love,

"August,
did you know you're
my Everything?"
said Big Fox one
evening.

"You tell me all the time!" said August.
"But what *is* Everything?"

"Oh, Everything is the best thing you could be. It's every new *flower* that blooms in spring."

"And every drop of *rain* that cools the summer."

"It's what it feels like to ride down the longest *hill* in the world. "

"Or to float up to
the highest clouds
in the *sky*."

"Everything is _warmer_ than the softest penguin in the snow."

"And **stronger**
than the tallest
llama in the jungle."

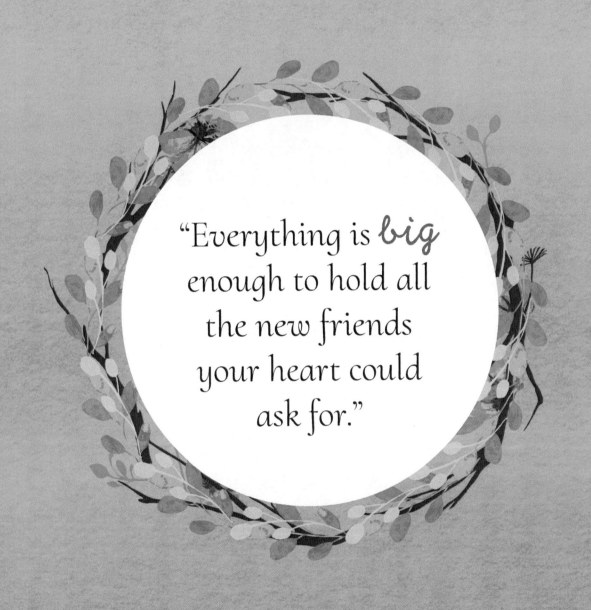

"Everything is *big* enough to hold all the new friends your heart could ask for."

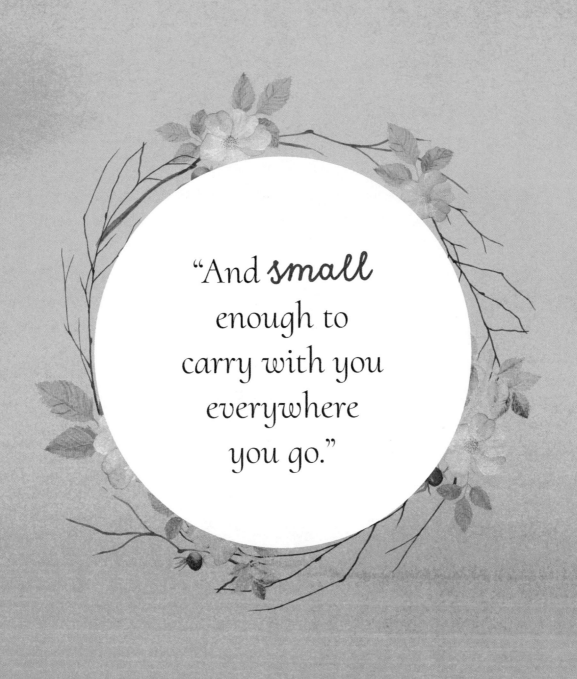

"And **small**
enough to
carry with you
everywhere
you go."

"Everything means, 'I love you with all my heart.' On your *happy* days . . ."

"... and on your *hard* days."

"And it means I will *always* be there during the long, long nights."

"Best of all,
Everything lasts
forever—longer,
even, than the longest
story that was ever
written."

"Wow," breathed
August. There
was a comforting
silence.

Then August whispered, "If
Everything means all that, then
you're my Everything, too."

Dearest August, you are my Everything in so many ways! Here are just a few:

_____

_____

_____

_____

_____

_____

_____

_____

_____

_____

_____

Cover and book design by David Miles

Visual credits: animal illustrations (Elena Barenbaum/Shutterstock.com); pink and green flower border (Karma3/Shutterstock.com); green leaves border (mika48/Shutterstock.com); colorful flower border (oksanka007/Shutterstock.com); yellow daisy flower border (TonTonic/Shutterstock.com); blue flower border (elsabenaa/Shutterstock.com); poppy flower border (OlgaVinokurova_art/Shutterstock.com); rose hip and twig flower border (Eisfrei/Shutterstock.com); fall flower border (Gluiki/Shutterstock.com); tropical flower border (Yana Fefelova/Shutterstock.com); snowflake border (Tokarchuk Andrii/Shutterstock.com); balloon border (Anastasia Lembrik/Shutterstock.com); apple flower border (julagaladriel/Shutterstock.com); raindrop border (Xansa/Shutterstock.com); red and blue flower border (Qvasimodo art/Shutterstock.com); clouds (Anna Konchits/Shutterstock.com); water puddle (Cute art/Shutterstock.com); cover stars (Margarita Manish/Shutterstock.com); cover star background (Anna Kutukova/Shutterstock.com); purple, red, and orange watercolor background (Jolliolly/Shutterstock.com); green and blue streaked watercolor background (Jolliolly/Shutterstock.com); green and blue watercolor background (Rennes/Shutterstock.com); cloud watercolor background (Magenta10/Shutterstock.com); blue watercolor background (Alyushin/Shutterstock.com); yellow and orange watercolor background (foxie/Shutterstock.com).

Made in the USA
Las Vegas, NV
07 November 2024

11172472R00021